Sleep Tight, Little Knight

GILLES TIBO
GENEVIÈVE DESPRÉS

Scholastic Canada Ltd.
Toronto New York London Auckland Sydney
Mexico City New Delhi Hong Kong Buenos Aires

To my lucky star . . .
— Gilles Tibo

For the once little Olivier, Thierry, Paul-Émile and Antonin.
— Geneviève Després

Scholastic Canada Ltd.
604 King Street West, Toronto, Ontario M5V 1E1, Canada

Scholastic Inc.
557 Broadway, New York, NY 10012, USA

Scholastic Australia Pty Limited
PO Box 579, Gosford, NSW 2250, Australia

Scholastic New Zealand Limited
Private Bag 94407, Botany, Manukau 2163, New Zealand

Scholastic Children's Books
Euston House, 24 Eversholt Street, London NW1 1DB, UK

www.scholastic.ca

Library and Archives Canada Cataloguing in Publication
Tibo, Gilles, 1951-
(Dors bien petit chevalier. English)
Sleep tight, little knight / Gilles Tibo ; illustrated by Geneviève
Després ; translated by Petra Johannson.
Translation of: Dors bien, petit chevalier.
ISBN 978-1-4431-7018-5 (softcover)
I. Després, Geneviève, illustrator II. Johannson, Petra, translator
III. Title. IV. Title: Dors bien petit chevalier. English.

PS8589.I26D6713 2019   jC843'.54   C2018-906404-8

6 5 4 3 2 1   Printed in Malaysia 108   19 20 21 22 23

The little knight is tired.

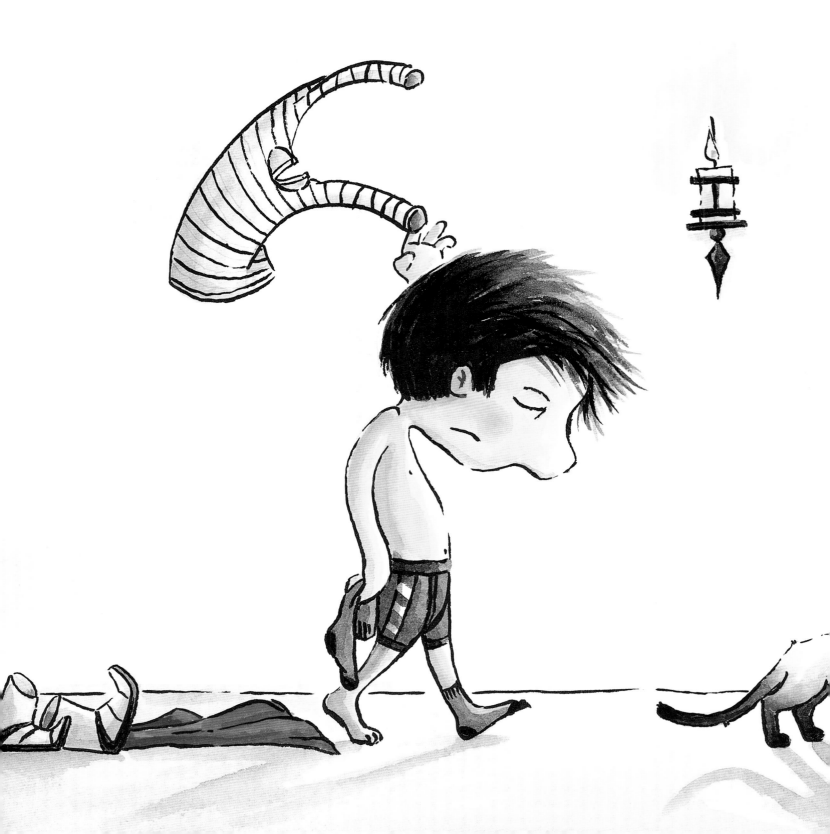

He brushes his teeth and gets ready for bed.

He puts on his favourite pyjamas and says goodnight to Bartlett.

Oh! A star has fallen out of the sky and onto his bed.

He tucks the star under his pillow.
"Goodnight, little star!"

The pointy ends prick
the little knight's ears,
so he tucks the star
under the covers.

But the star pricks his belly.

How will he ever get to sleep?

There. That should do it.

Finally, the little knight
falls fast asleep.